My Baby-sitter

For Mabel MacDeavitt

VIKING KESTREL

Viking Penguin Inc., 40 West 23rd Street, New York, New York 10010, U.S.A.

Penguin Books Ltd, Harmondsworth, Middlesex, England

Penguin Books Australia Ltd, Ringwood, Victoria, Australia

Penguin Books Canada Limited, 2801 John Street, Markham, Ontario, Canada L3R 1B4

Penguin Books (N.Z.) Ltd, 182–190 Wairau Road, Auckland 10, New Zealand

First published in 1987 by Viking Penguin Inc.

Published simultaneously in Canada

Manufactured in Singapore by Imago Publishing Ltd.

Set in Garamond #3

1   2   3   4   5   91   90   89   88   87

Library of Congress Cataloging in Publication Data

Young, Ruth, 1946–   My babysitter.

Summary: A child's enjoyable afternoon with the babysitter is full of games to play, stories to tell, and pictures

to draw to surprise Mommy when she comes home.

[1. Baby sitters—Fiction]   I. Title.

II. Title: My babysitter.   PZ7.Y877My   1987   [E]   87-6220   ISBN 0-670-81305-2

My Baby-sitter

RUTH YOUNG

VIKING KESTREL

This afternoon when Mommy goes out, my baby-sitter will come.

Her name is Marcella.
She always wears a hat.

We say good-bye to Mommy at the door.
"Good-bye, Mommy. See you later!"

We tell stories.

We blow bubbles.

We play puppets.

Sometimes we make music with glasses of water!

I wear Marcella's sunglasses.
Marcella makes chocolate pudding.

We like to eat it still a little bit hot but not too hot.

"Hello, Mommy!"